INSPECTOR NOAH AND HIS SUPER SLEUTH DOG WATSON'S
JUNGLE ADVENTURE

Author: Kallie Caton

This book belongs to:

_____

"Kallie Caton"

Welcome to the colorful world of
Inspector Noah and Watson's Jungle Adventure!
As you embark on this exciting journey with
Our brave duo, feel free to add your own
Colors and creativity to the pages. Make this book
Uniquely yours and let your imagination soar.
Happy coloring and happy adventures!

Illustrations by Sabaanwer

Dedication

Dedication Page:

For my grandson Noah and his dog Watson,

This book is dedicated to all the adventurers,
dreamers, and explorers who find joy in
unraveling mysteries, big and small.
From the depths of the
sea to the vastness of the desert,
and even to the far reaches of space,
may you always have the courage to embark
on exciting journeys like Inspector Noah
and Watson's Jungle Adventure.
Keep exploring, keep dreaming, and
never stop believing in the magic of discovery.

By: Kallie Caton

Table of Contents:

In a world of wonder,
Where mysteries unfold,
Lived Inspector Noah,
Brave and bold.
With his Super Sleuth Dog,
Watson by his side,
They set off on an adventure,
With courage and pride.

Through the dense jungle,
They ventured deep,
Looking for Hippo,
Who might be asleep.
With Watson's keen senses and
Noah's bright eyes,
They searched for clues
Under the endless skies.

They came upon a path,overgrown and wild,
And though it seemed daunting,
They both smiled.
For with Watson's nose and Noah's quick wit,
They were ready to solve the mystery,
Bit by bit.

Through thick vines and tangled trees,
They followed the trail,
With the greatest of ease.
With each step forward,
they felt a little nearer,
A lake! So calm it looked like a mirror.

But suddenly,
A ripple traveled across the water,
Caught their attention,
As they looked even farther.
With Watson's ears perked and Noah's heart strong.

They followed the ripple,
how could they have known,
As Watson stepped on what
he thought was a stone.
Then up popped Hippo, Watson sitting upright.
Mystery solved! Hippo was alright.

With Watson's keen senses
And Noah's steadfast grace,
They solved the mystery, in that wondrous place.
And as they journeyed back under the sky so blue,
Their adventure was only beginning, what a crew!

So here's to Inspector Noah
And Watson, a duo so fine,
Whose adventures will echo through space and time.
With courage and friendship, they'll always do best,
Noah and Watson , being so blessed.

Welcome to the Inspiration Page!

Congratulations on completing Inspector
Noah and Watson's Jungle Adventure!
As you flip through the colorful pages
You've filled with your imagination,
Remember that the adventure
Doesn't have to end here.
Let this book inspire you to explore
New worlds, embark on exciting
Journeys, and create your own stories.

Just like Inspector Noah and Watson,
You have the courage and curiosity to discover
The wonders of the world around you.
Whether it's exploring the depths of a jungle,
Solving mysteries, or simply embracing
The beauty of nature, the possibilities are endless.

So, grab your crayons, let your creativity
Soar, and never stop believing in
The magic of imagination.
Who knows what amazing adventures await you next?
The journey is yours to create.

Thank you for joining us on this adventure.
Remember,
The greatest stories are the ones we write ourselves.

Coloring Tips Page:

Choose Colors Wisely: Pick colors you love that fit the jungle theme.
Start Light, Build Up: Begin lightly and layer colors for depth.
Blend and Experiment: Try blending colors for unique effects.
Stay Organized: Keep supplies handy for easy access.
Take Your Time: Relax and enjoy the process; there's no rush.
Have Fun: Let your imagination run wild and enjoy the adventure!

Draw Hippo

Draw your favorite animal.

Help Inspector Noah
Find his way through the
Jungle maze to reach Hippo's hiding spot!

Parent Notes

Parent Notes

THE END

Made in United States
Troutdale, OR
10/27/2024

24181341R00017